Pretzel and the Puppies

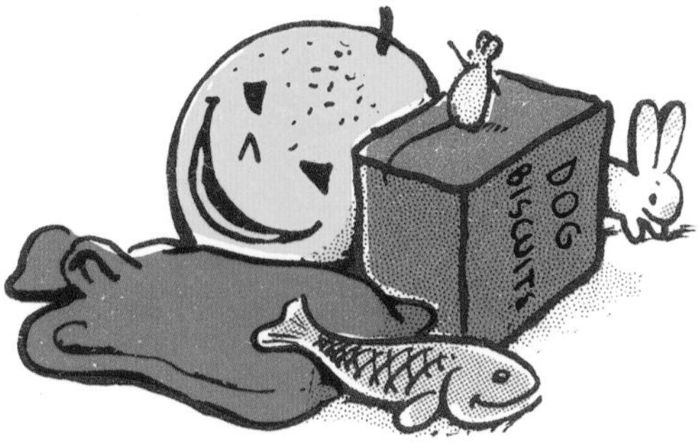
DOG
BISCUITS

by

Margret & H. A. Rey

Houghton Mifflin Harcourt
Boston New York

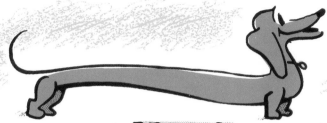

This is **PRETZEL**,
the longest dachshund in the world.
He can do many things because he is so long,
but it does not always turn out well...

This is **GRETA**, Pretzel's wife.
She sometimes has to straighten things out
when Pretzel gets into trouble.

POLLY   PENNY   PAT   PETE   PUCK

These are the **PUPPIES**
(two girls and three boys), who love to
play with their Daddy.

And if you want to know more about Pretzel—

— just turn the page!

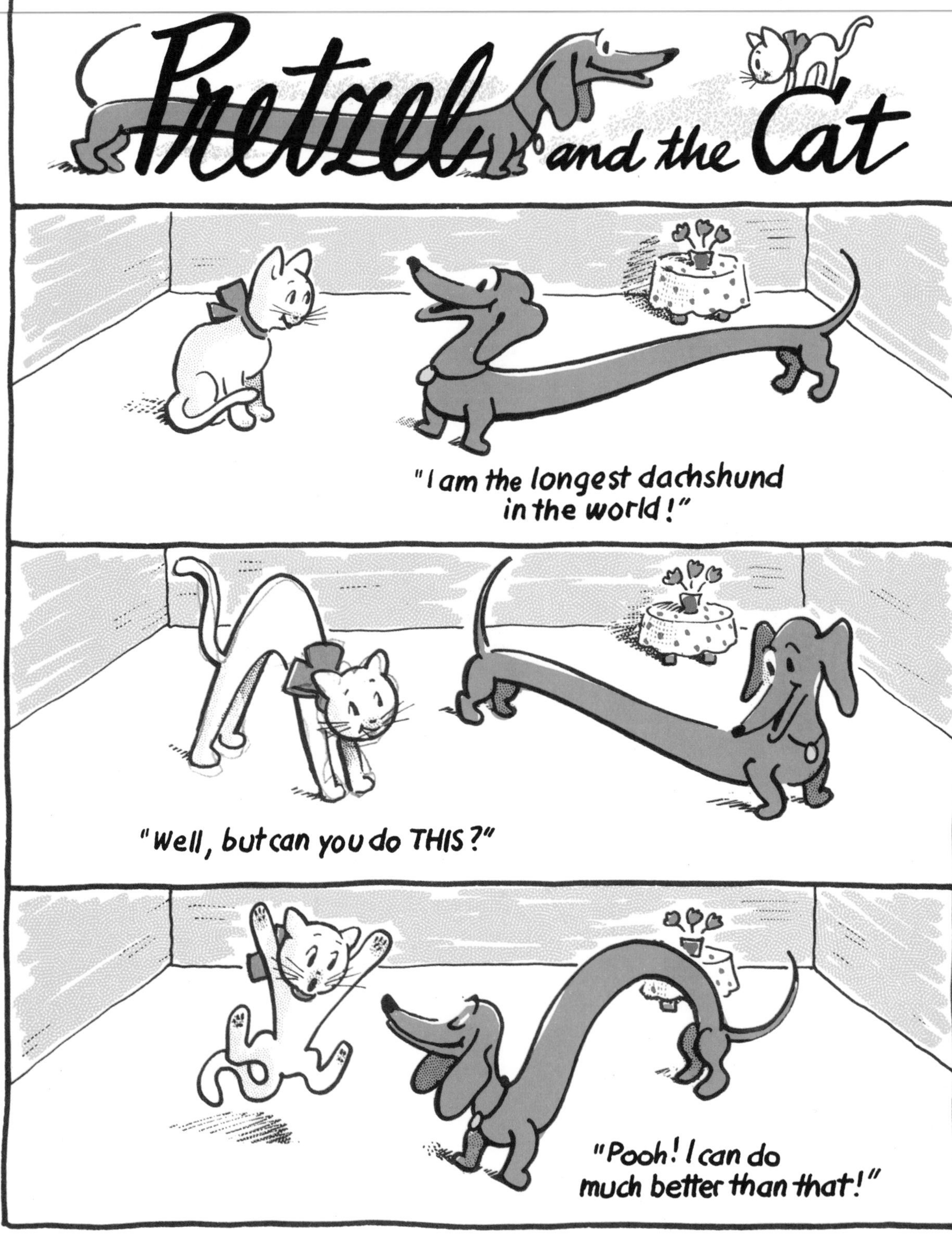
Pretzel and the Cat
"I am the longest dachshund in the world!"
"Well, but can you do THIS?"
"Pooh! I can do much better than that!"

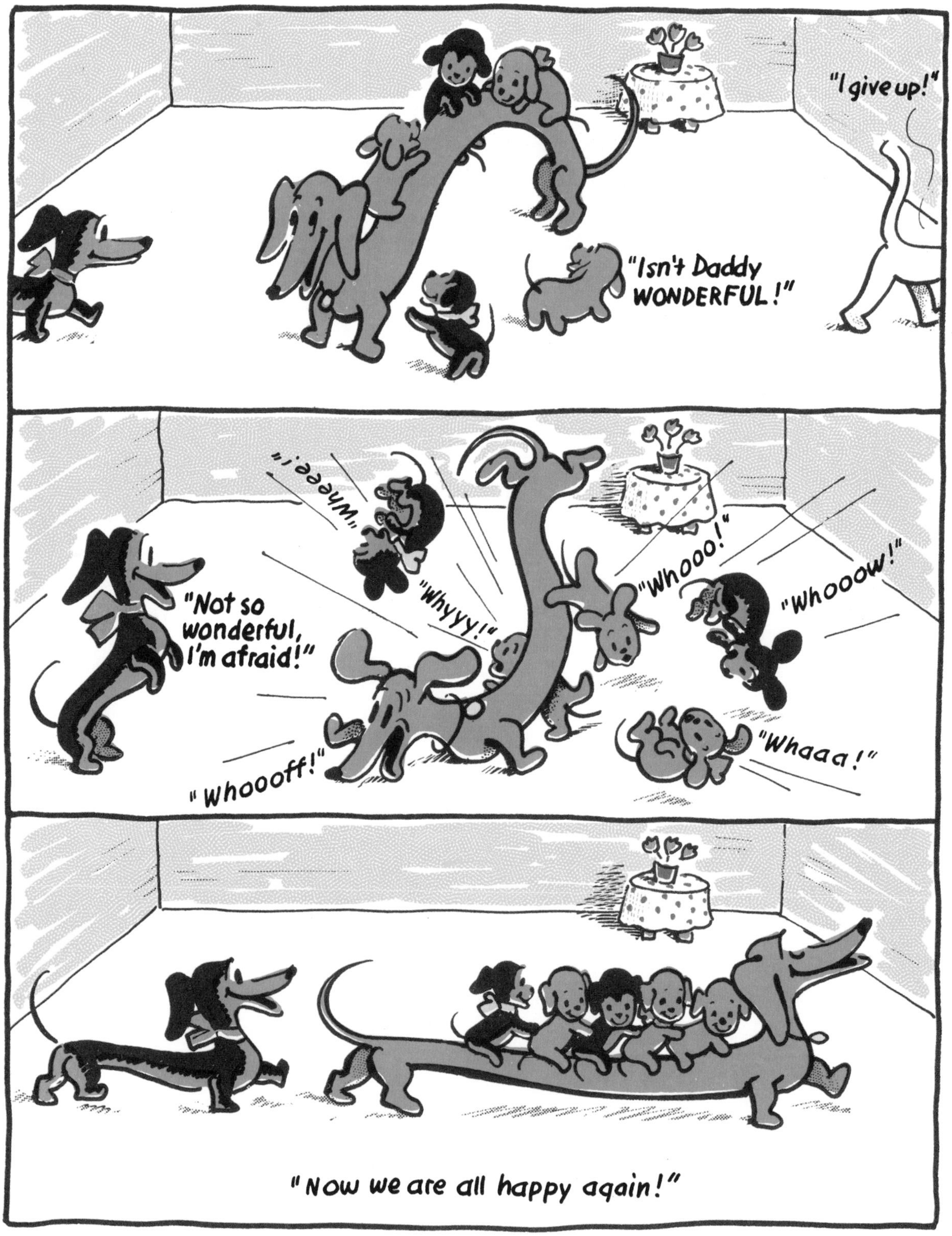
"Isn't Daddy WONDERFUL!"
"I give up!"
"Not so wonderful, I'm afraid!"
"Wheee!"
"Whyyy!"
"Whooo!"
"Whooow!"
"Whoooff!"
"Whaaa!"
"Now we are all happy again!"

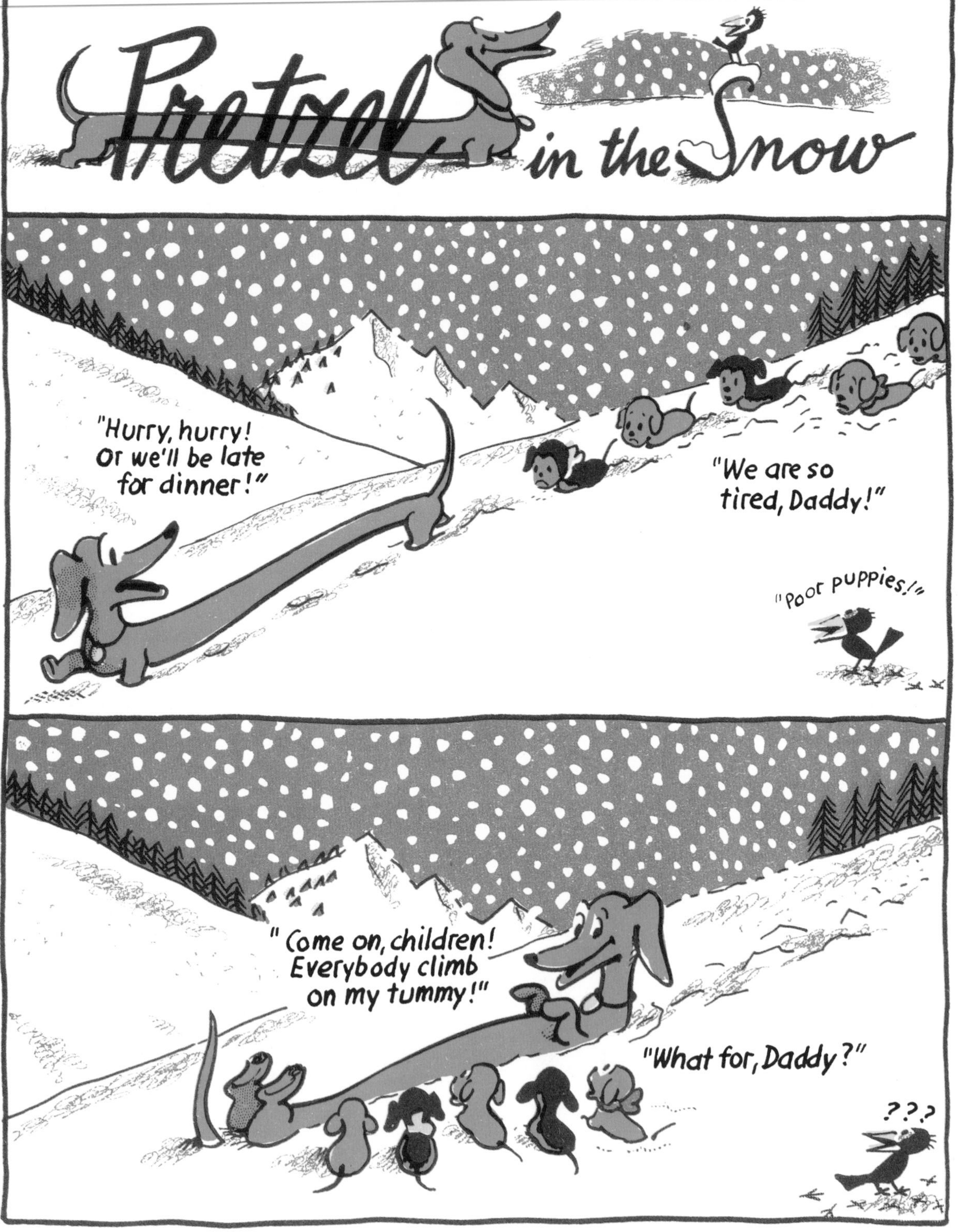
Pretzel in the Snow
"Hurry, hurry! Or we'll be late for dinner!"
"We are so tired, Daddy!"
"Poor puppies!"
"Come on, children! Everybody climb on my tummy!"
"What for, Daddy?"
???

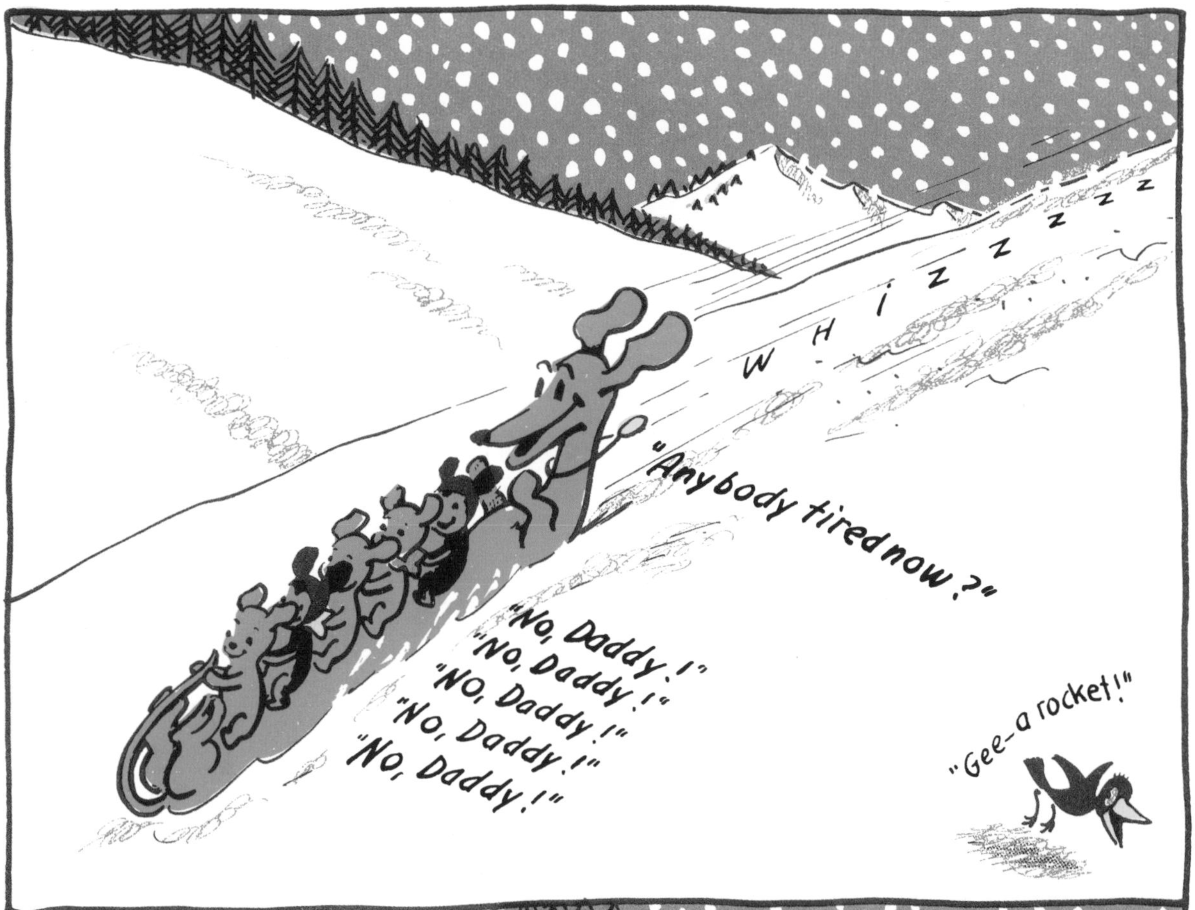
WHIZZZZZZZ
"Anybody tired now?"
"No, Daddy!"
"No, Daddy!"
"No, Daddy!"
"No, Daddy!"
"No, Daddy!"
"Gee—a rocket!"

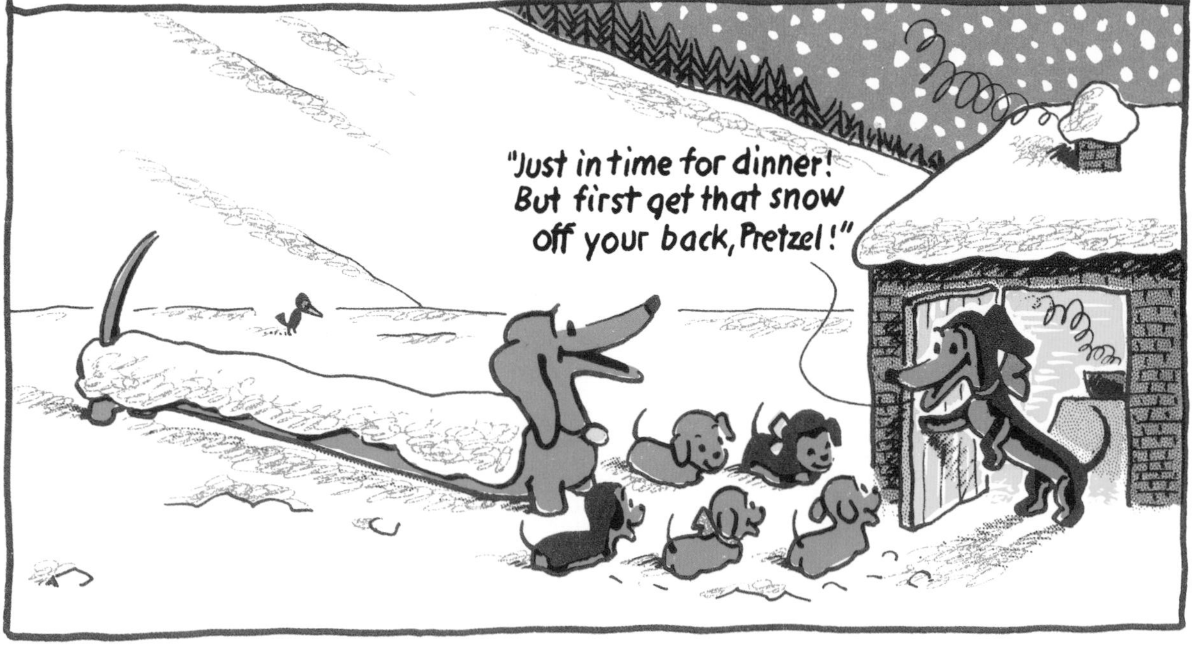
"Just in time for dinner! But first get that snow off your back, Pretzel!"

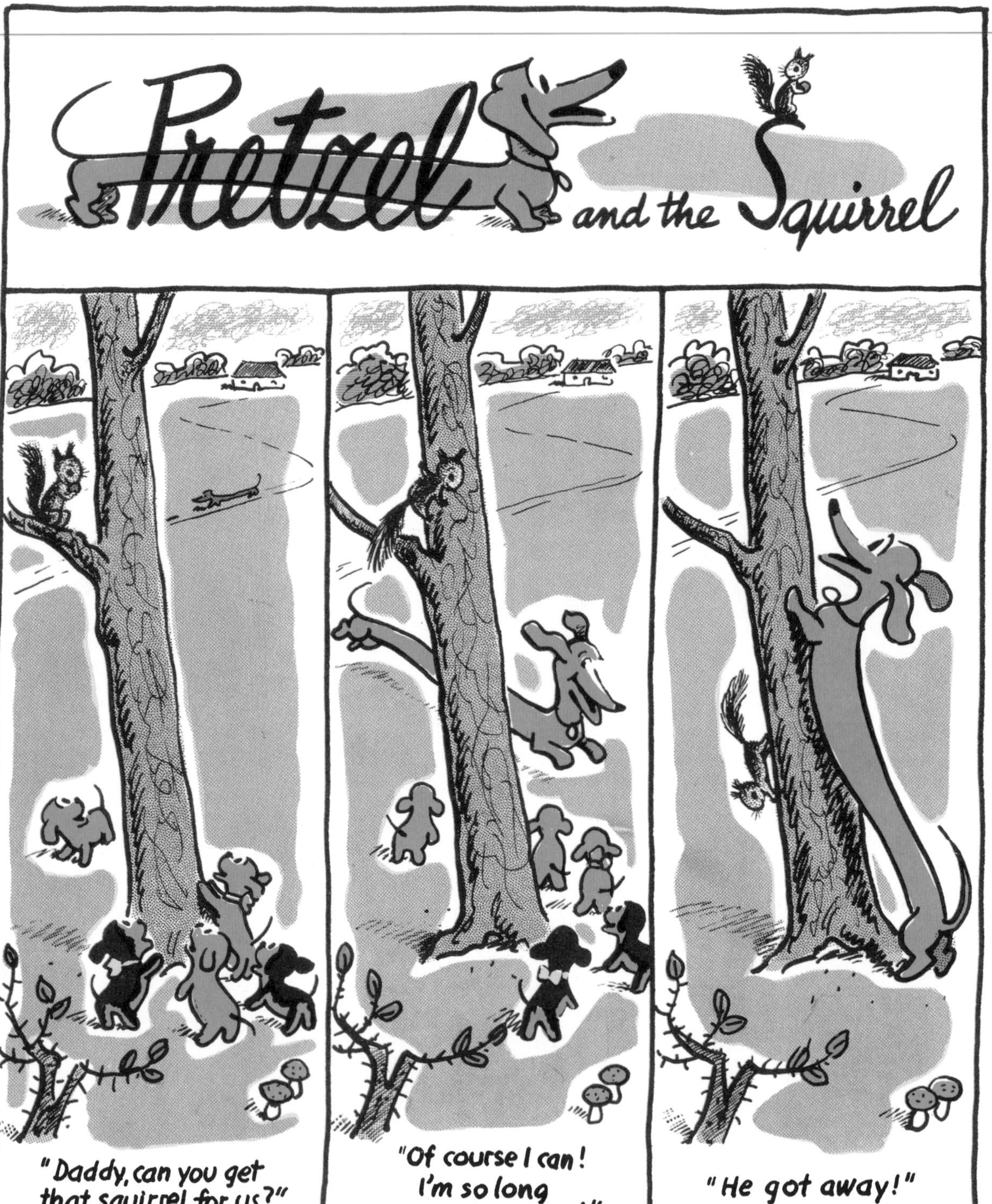
Pretzel and the Squirrel
"Daddy, can you get that squirrel for us?"
"Of course I can! I'm so long I can reach him!"
"He got away!"

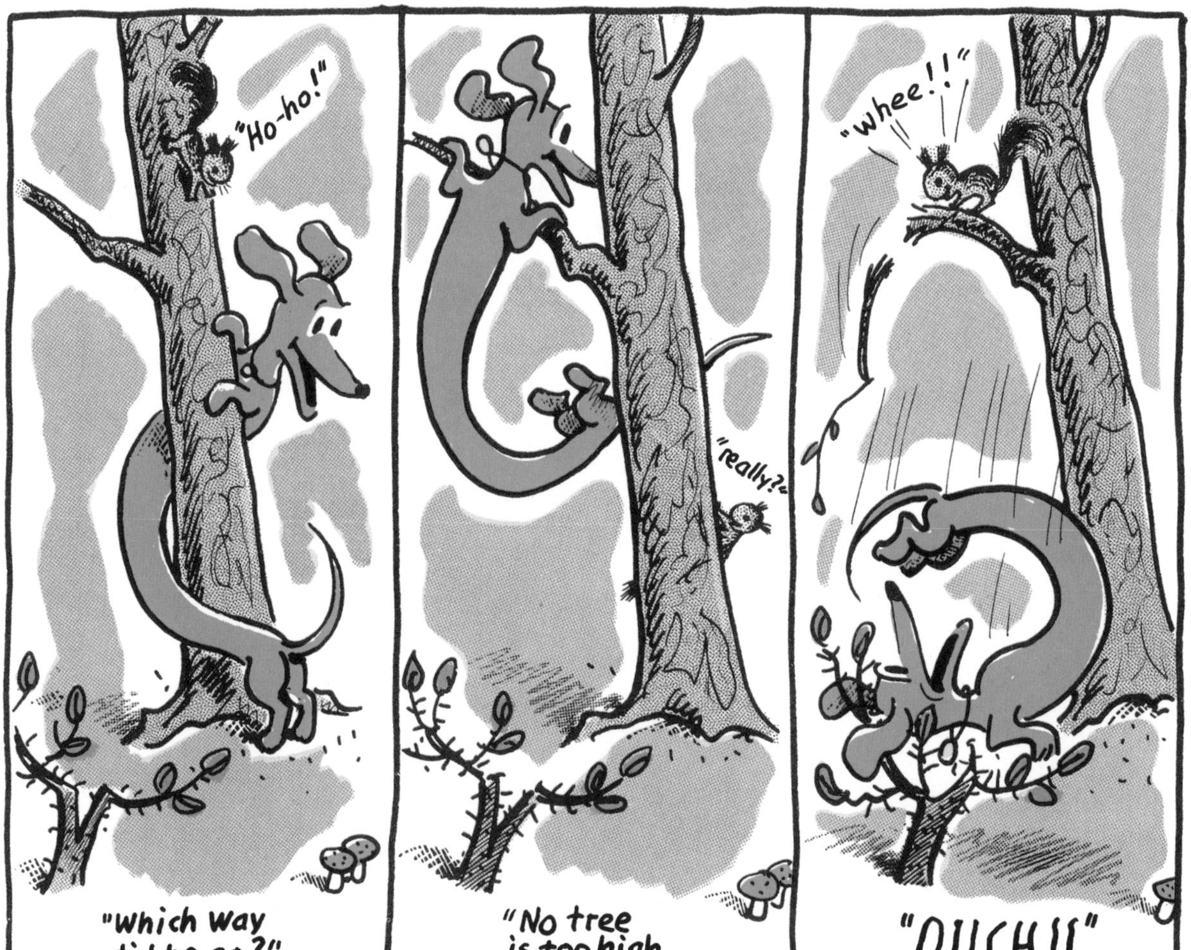
"Ho-ho!"
"Which way did he go?"
"No tree is too high for ME!"
"really?"
"whee!!"
"OUCH!!"
"Nasty squirrel, wasn't it?"
"Poor Daddy-he looks like a porcupine!"
"It's your own fault, Pretzel! Just being LONG isn't everything!"

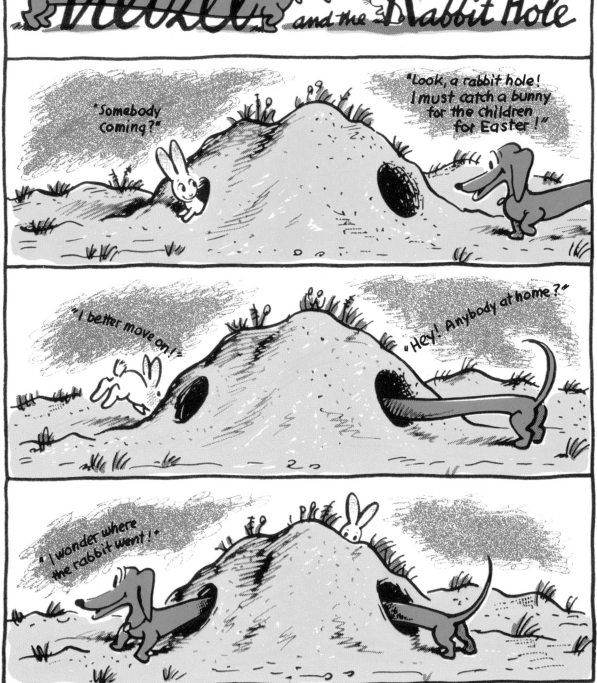

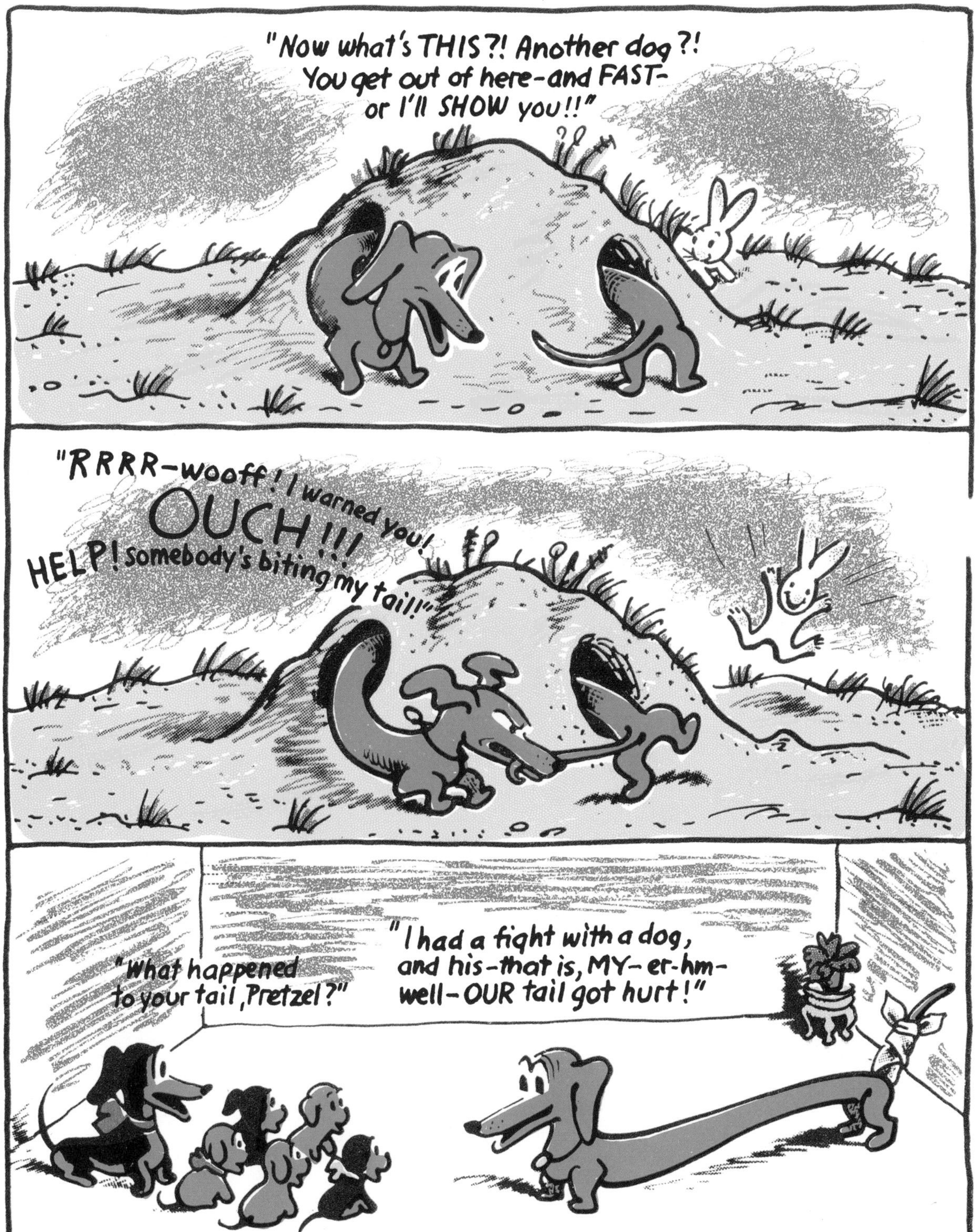
"Now what's THIS?! Another dog?! You get out of here-and FAST- or I'll SHOW you!!"
"RRRR-wooff! I warned you!
OUCH!!!
HELP! somebody's biting my tail!"
"What happened to your tail, Pretzel?"
"I had a fight with a dog, and his-that is, MY-er-hm-well-OUR tail got hurt!"

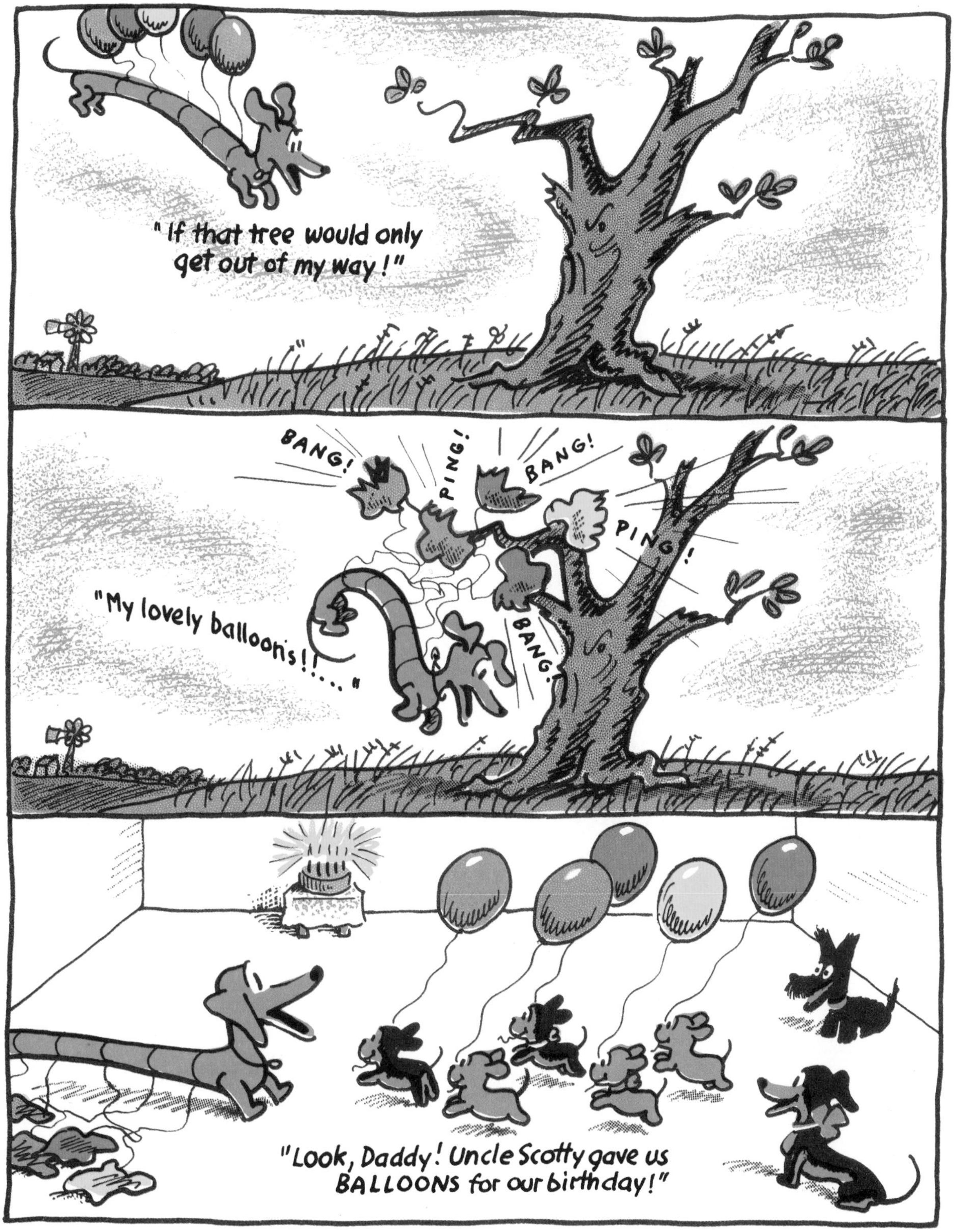
"If that tree would only get out of my way!"
BANG!
PING!
BANG!
PING!!
BANG.
"My lovely balloons!!...."
"Look, Daddy! Uncle Scotty gave us BALLOONS for our birthday!"

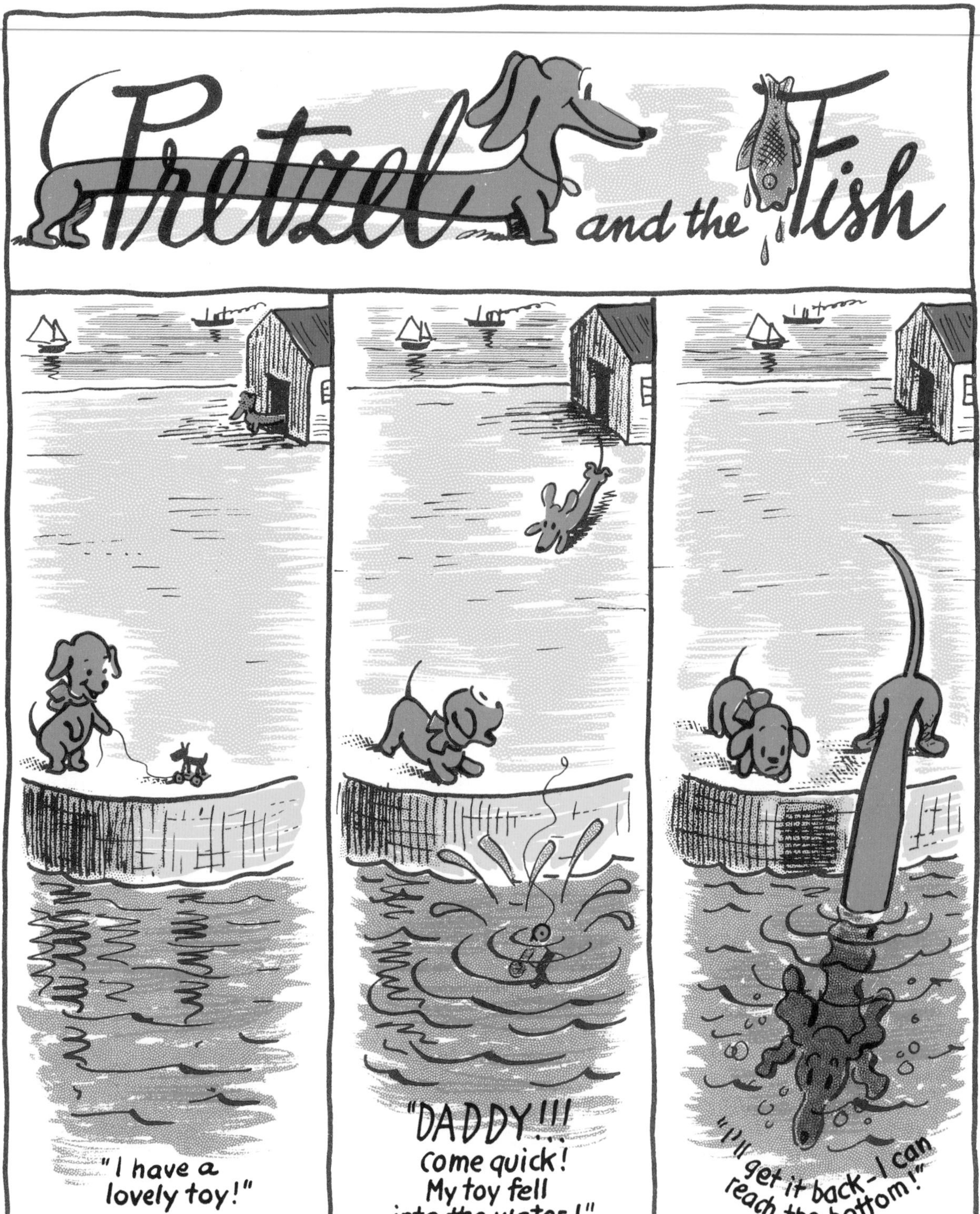
Pretzel and the Fish
"I have a lovely toy!"
"DADDY!!! come quick! My toy fell into the water!"
"I'll get it back—I can reach the bottom!"

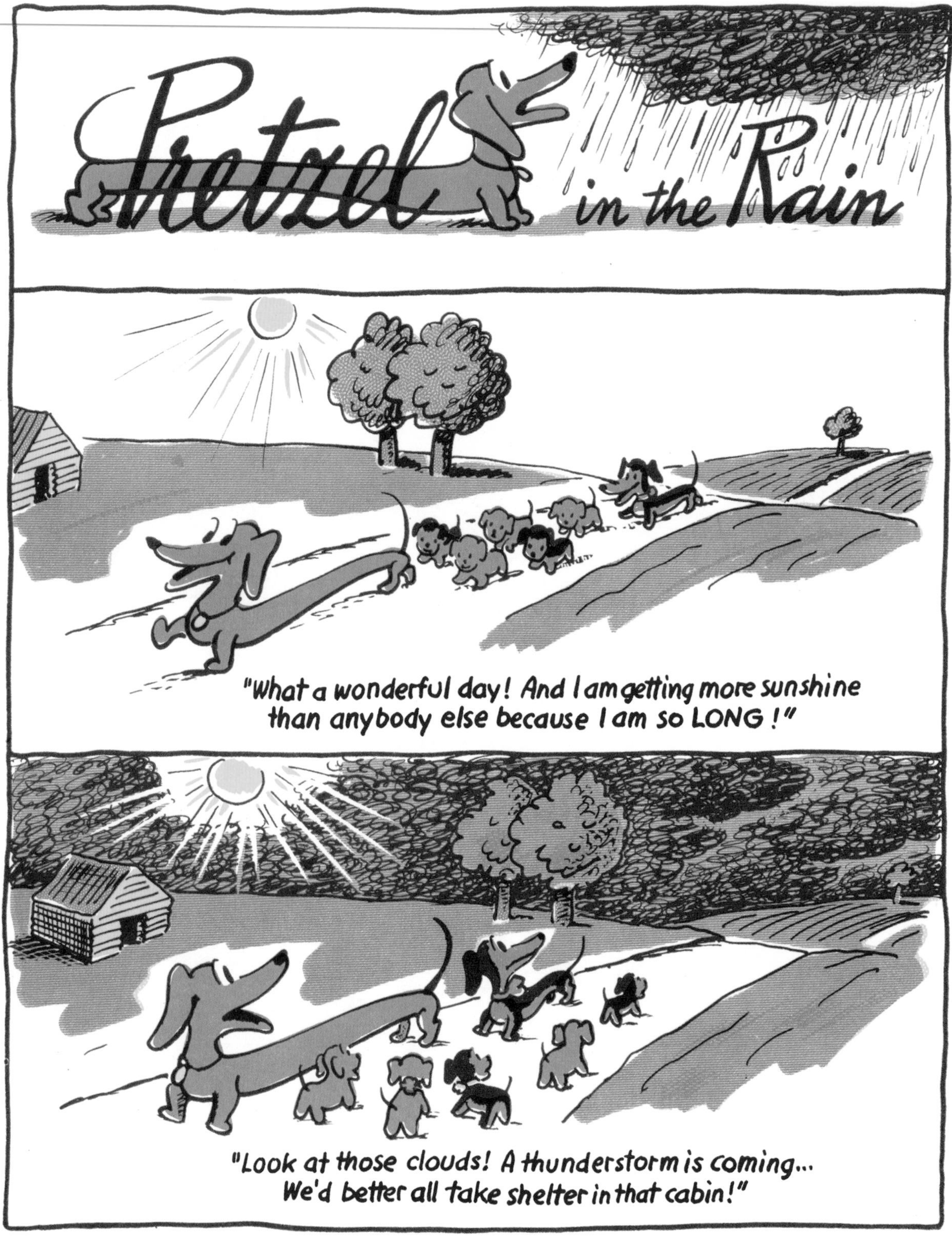
Pretzel in the Rain
"What a wonderful day! And I am getting more sunshine than anybody else because I am so LONG!"
"Look at those clouds! A thunderstorm is coming... We'd better all take shelter in that cabin!"

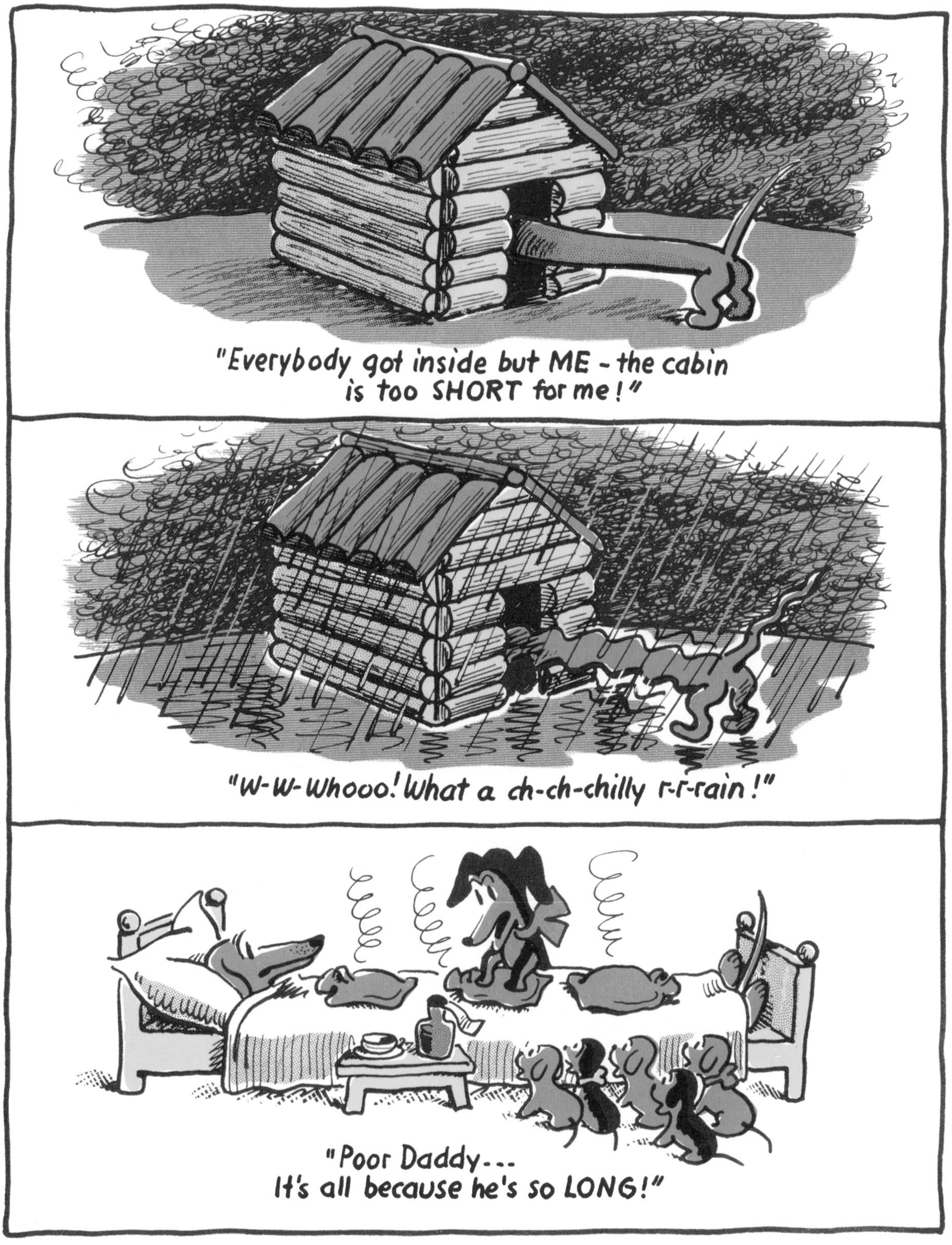
"Everybody got inside but ME - the cabin is too SHORT for me!"
"W-W-Whooo! What a ch-ch-chilly r-r-rain!"
"Poor Daddy...
It's all because he's so LONG!"

"Here's the list of the groceries, Pretzel!
You better take the children along to help you carry them!"

"I don't need any help –
I'm so long I can carry it all by myself!"

"A MOUSE!
I must catch him!
Perhaps it's the one who was at our cheese last week?!"

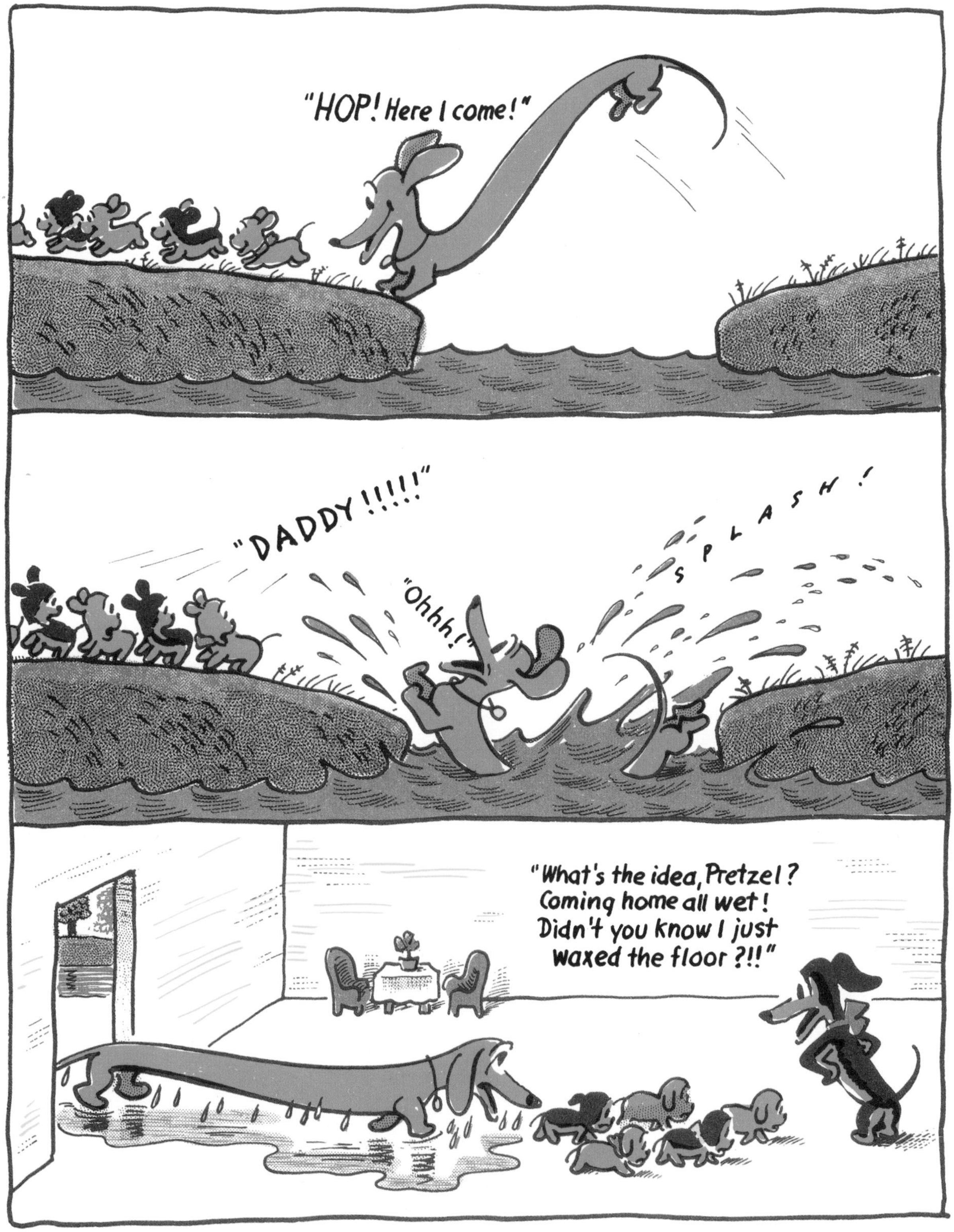
"HOP! Here I come!"
"DADDY!!!!!"
"Ohhh!"
SPLASH!
"What's the idea, Pretzel? Coming home all wet! Didn't you know I just waxed the floor?!!"

Pretzel in the Chimney

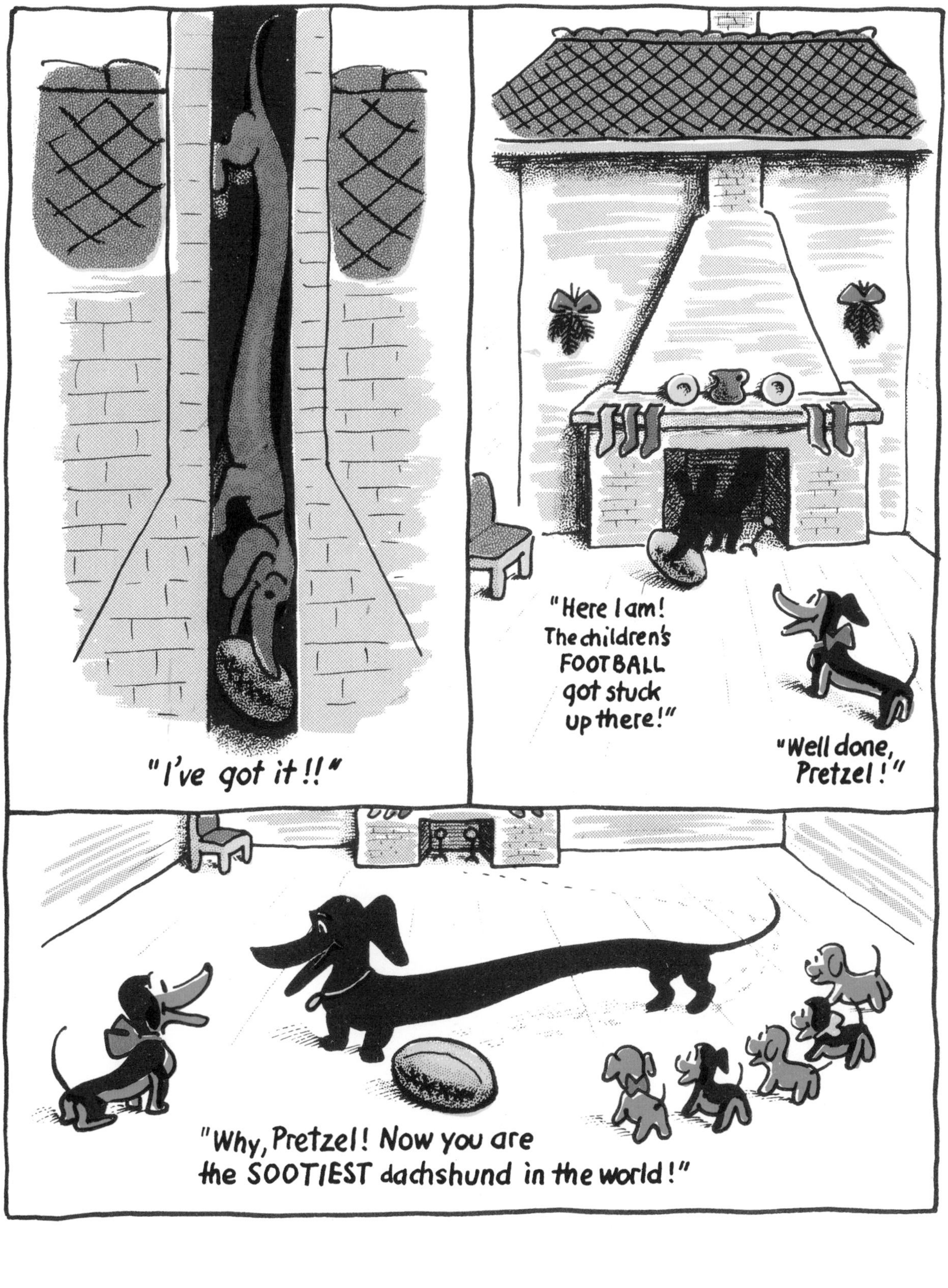
"I've got it!!"
"Here I am! The children's FOOTBALL got stuck up there!"
"Well done, Pretzel!"
"Why, Pretzel! Now you are the SOOTIEST dachshund in the world!"

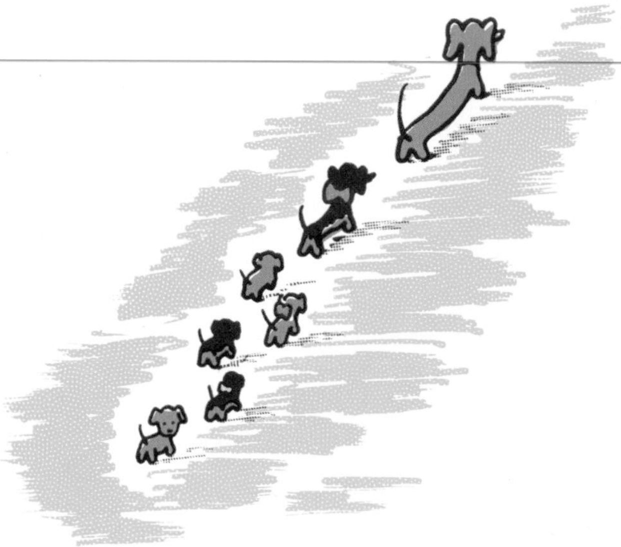

That's all -

goodbye!

Originally published in hardcover by Harper & Brothers, 1946.

For information about permission to reproduce selections from this book, write to trade.permissions@hmhco.com or to Permissions, Houghton Mifflin Harcourt Publishing Company, 3 Park Avenue, 19th Floor, New York, New York 10016.

hmhbooks.com

The text of this book is hand lettered.

ISBN: 978-0-358-46826-4 hardcover
ISBN: 978-0-358-65959-4 paperback

Printed in Italy
1
4500836211